For my mother and father,
Morwenna and Thomas, who took me
round the world and taught me
how to swim
S.P

To Kate - with love
S.L.

British Library Cataloguing Publication Data
A catalogue record of this book is available from the British Library

HB ISBN 0 340 72407 2
PB ISBN 0 340 72408 0

First hb edition published 2000
First pb edition published 2000

1 3 5 7 9 10 8 6 4 2

Published in 2000 by Hodder Children's Books,
a division of Hodder Headline,
338 Euston Road, London NW1 3BH

Edited by Kate Burns
Designed by Dawn Apperley

Printed in Hong Kong

Coral Goes Swimming

Simon Puttock and Stephen Lambert

Hodder
Children's
Books

A division of Hodder Headline

It was a hot day. Dad was busy indoors.
'Why not run along outside and play?'
he said to Coral.

The water in the paddling pool rippled and slooped invitingly.

Coral splashed and swooshed about. The water was lovely. She practised floating and her knees stuck out of the water like mountains out of the middle of a sea.

'I'm just like an island in a great big ocean,' thought Coral, and she lay back and let the water begin to carry her away.

It floated her along past other people's back gardens, past shops and car-parks, past roads and factories . . . all the way down to the sea.

Out at sea the waves were
quite big but Coral was a
good swimmer.
She swam down the Channel
between Britain and France.
Seagulls squawked overhead and
people on the crowded decks of
a ferry smiled and waved.

She crossed the Bay of Biscay
and turned the corner of Spain.
Coral kept swimming.

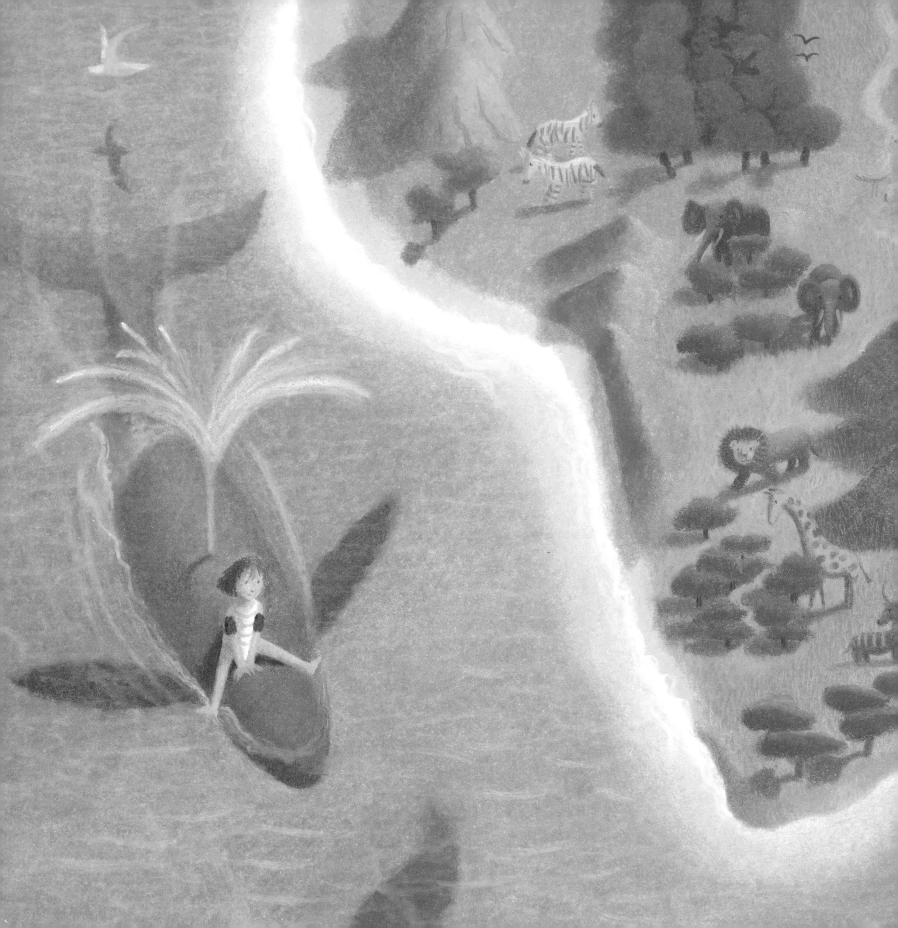

Coral swam right round Africa.
It was hard going at the Cape of
Good Hope; the waves were as
big as sea-monsters. But whales
even bigger than the waves
came spouting by to keep
her company.

They looped the loop round
Madagascar . . .

In the Indian Ocean, Coral trod
water which was so clear she
could see crabs and lobsters
creeping over the sandy
ocean floor.
A million bright and tiny fishes
flashed between her feet and a
family of seahorses sailed
gracefully by.

Coral said goodbye to the whales
and kept swimming, past the
exotic islands of Indonesia.

From the bottom of Australia, Coral saw the tiny tips of distant icebergs. Penguins flip-flap flew underwater, chasing their dinner through the chilly deep.

The Pacific Ocean was very big.

Coral swam and saw flying fish as she passed Fiji. She swam and swam and saw turtles at Tahiti.

Then she swam and swam and swam until she almost bumped her nose on the coast of California where seals were playing at tag. Coral played with them in the bubbling surf until . . .

. . . the fearsome fin of a tiger shark came cutting through the water.

'Yikes!' said Coral and swam south.

She swam so fast that Mexico and Ecuador, Peru and long, skinny Chile flashed by.

She swam so fast the shark gave up the chase. Out of breath, Coral rounded Cape Horn.

'Phew!' said Coral and, feeling tired, she let her water-wings hold her up as she drifted north with the warm current, past Argentina and Brazil.

'Mmmm,' said Coral.

Coral lay back and relaxed past Caribbean islands.

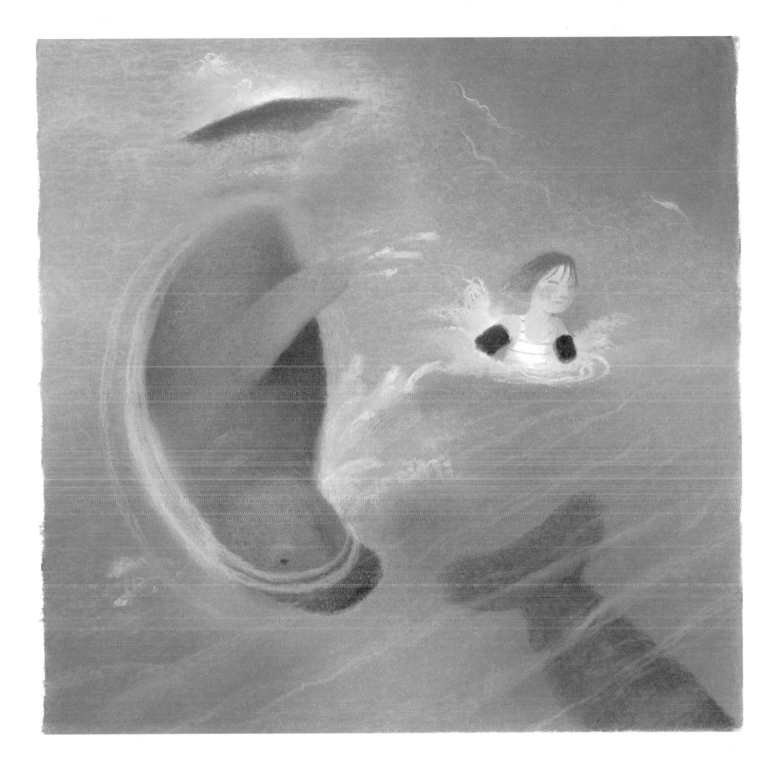

As she floated by Florida, a manatee snorted and flipped foam at her. Coral stopped to play but the manatee slipped shyly away, so Coral kept on swimming.

She got a bit tangled up in smelly seaweed in
the wide Sargasso sea, so she clambered
out and walked on it.
Carefully, she trod round little crabs that
nipped their pinchers at her.
Eels wriggled through the weed and
between her toes which made her
feet feel funny.
Coral swam the last lap home through the
great, grey-green Atlantic swell.

'It's time to come in now, Coral. Supper's ready.'
Dad gave Coral a nice, big, towely hug.
'Let's not drip all over the rug,' he said. 'Oh, look, you're all pruney.'

Coral ate her tea in record time.
It was Dad's Special Summer Salad with Thousand Island dressing.
She was so hungry she had two big helpings of Baked Alaska Pudding.
'Did you enjoy your paddle, love?' said Dad. 'You certainly worked up an appetite!'

When it was time for bed, the first stars
were appearing in the evening sky.
'Just like sparkles in a deep, blue sea,'
thought Coral, and she closed her eyes
and lay back in her bed and let the blue,
sparkling night begin to carry her away . . .

Can you follow Coral's route around the world?

ARCTIC OCEAN

United Kingdom

NORTH AMERICA

EUROPE

Sargasso Sea

ATLANTIC OCEAN

AFRICA

Caribbean

PACIFIC OCEAN

SOUTH AMERICA

Cape

Cape Horn

ASIA

INDONESIAN Islands

Madagascar

INDIAN OCEAN

AUSTRALASIA

od Hope